Jason
Cockcr

h
Hodder
Children's
Books
A division of Hodder Headline plc

PET

In the whole realm of Fairyland and in all the sunlit world there was no man so handsome as Tamlin. He could have captured the heart of any princess with his golden hair and ready smile. So many wondered (and one of them was Tamlin) why he chose Janet for his sweetheart. Plain Janet.

Be that as it may, one day among the red roses of her garden, they kissed. And Tamlin and Janet might have married on Midsummer's Eve . . . but for what happened.

One sunny day, when Tamlin was out riding, his horse shied at a flash of light, and Tamlin fell and struck his head.

Dizzy and dazed, it seemed to him that a lady came riding to his aid, her horse's mane strung with silver bells. Her dress was green silk, her cloak of green velvet, and she reached down to him a soft, white hand.

"Up, Tamlin, and share my saddle," she said, "and I shall take you home where you belong."

The ground turned blood red. They had crossed into Fairyland where the blood of all the world's wars runs ankle-deep.

And though the Queen gave Tamlin shoes of green velvet and a coat of fine wool, a white mare to ride, and more kisses than he cared to take, she would not give him his freedom, no, not for love nor money.

When Tamlin's horse came home without its rider, Janet plaited her red hair, pulled on her cloak, and searched. She searched the Ettrick and Yarrow, searched by the holy well, among the snowberries and among the red broom. But she found no trace of her sweetheart. Janet went to her garden - to the rose garden where she and Tamlin had kissed. And there she picked a double rose - two roses on one stem. Throwing one aside, she spoke to the other: "Now tell me, my love. What must I do?" When the rose had finished speaking, all its petals fell at Janet's feet.

Janet went to her Father and said: "Farewell, Daddy. I am going to fetch me home my Tamlin, for I fear he has fallen into the hands of the Fairies and cannot save himself."

"What? Steal out on Hallowe'en, when all the demons and witches of the world are loose and roaming? Any other

night of the year, Janet! Don't travel out tonight!"

But her mind was made up. She rode over Ettrick and Yarrow, past red broom and yellow, to the crossroads at Milescross, half a league from Fairyland. And there she hid herself in a bush and waited for midnight and the Witching Hour.

What did she see, that Hallowe'en?
Bats and black cats, and a skeleton
dancing in the wind. She saw the
gravestones heave and the moss
crawl, heard banshee laughter
drifting on the wind. A dark shape
sped across the moon, and the
owls jabbered in strange languages:
babbled and sang and wept. The
wind moaned and the trees groaned,
and the foggy dew rested like a
clammy hand on Janet's forehead.
Then at last, at midnight, she heard
it: the distant jingling of bridles.

Along the road came a company of riders led by a lady on an elfin horse.
Fifty-nine bells caught the moonlight - like a cloud of silver bubbles.
Behind the Fairy Queen rode a man on a jet black horse.
Janet's heart beat faster . . . but the feet in the stirrups
were hooves, and the man was not Tamlin.
Behind him rode a man on a chestnut mare.
Janet's heart beat faster still . . . but the hands on
the reins were furry, and the man was not Tamlin.
Behind him rode a man on a dapple grey.
Janet's heart skipped a beat . . . but the face
under the hood had a great black beard,
and the man was not Tamlin.

Hidden in her bush, Janet watched
them all pass - all handsome men.
But when a milk-white mare
crossed the moonlit crossroads, she
leapt at once from her hiding place
and seized his fine wool cloak,
dragging him from the saddle, saying,
"Tamlin, I have you, and I shall
never let go!"
The Fairy Queen reined in her
horse and looked back. She saw
Janet roll Tamlin in her arms and
hold him by the hair. And the Queen
only laughed at the girl's foolishness.
"Oh, you will let go soon enough,
Plain Janet, when you see what
magic can do!"

All at once Tamlin's scalp grew cold and scaley to the touch, and
Janet found in her arms not a man but a lizard, cold as clay, with
bulging, swivelling eyes. She screamed . . .
but she did not let go. "You may change,
but I am true," she said, gripping its
lizard frill. "You are my Tamlin
and I shall never let go!"

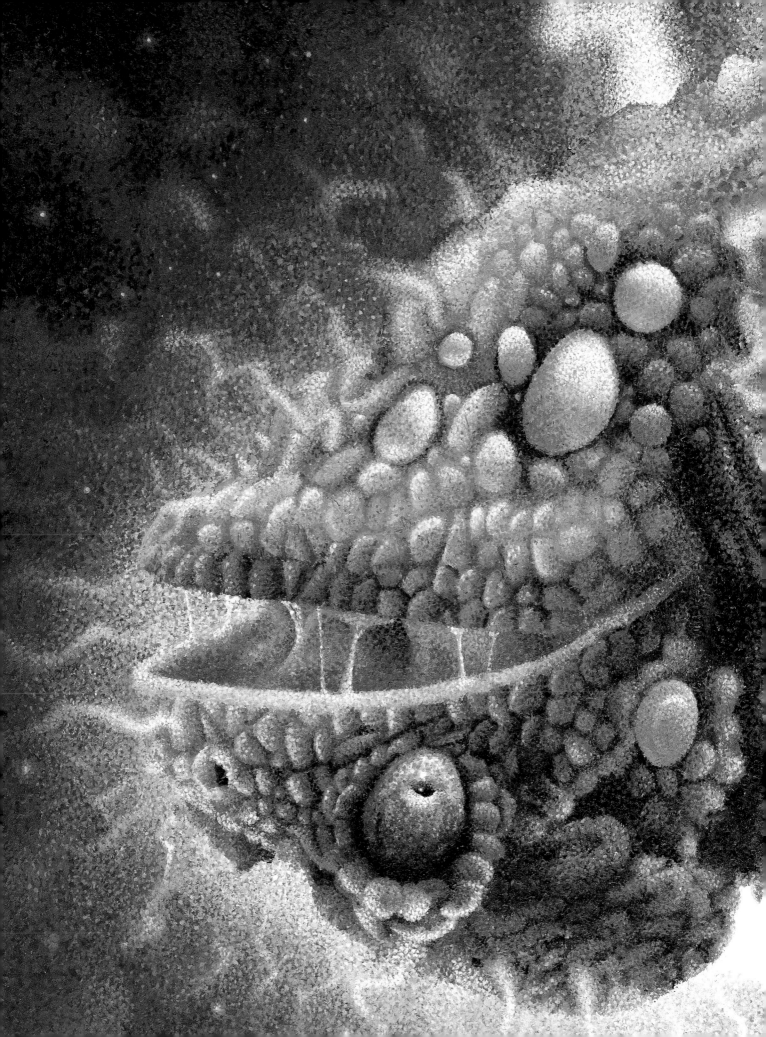

The lizard lashed its armoured tail, then coiled itself around her. Its thick rough body shrank to the slippery thinness of a hose, but its length doubled, and a forked tongue flickered in her face. Janet found in her arms not a lizard but a snake. She shuddered as the coils entwined her . . . but she did not let go.

"You may change, but I am true," she said. "You are my Tamlin, and I shall never let you go!"

Fairy eyes glittered all around, watching, watching.

The snake in her arms put on fur. It stood up, lifting Janet in giant furry paws, claws flashing in the moonlight. No longer was Janet holding a snake in her arms: she was held, instead, in the arms of a bear!

Burying her fingers deep in his shaggy shawl, she bellowed in the bear's ear: "You may change, but I am true. You are my Tamlin, and I shall never let go!"

The bear deafened her with its growl - a growl which crumbled like an avalanche into a roar.

The fur in her fingers turned golden yellow and the bear turned into a lion. Still Janet did not let go.

The lion was transformed into a horse, which tossed her high into the frosty air - struck sparks from the ground with its silver shoes, carried her, at a gallop, round the gibbet and the black thorn tree and back again. But Janet kept tight hold of its mane, crying, "I shall never let go!"

Somewhere, a church clock struck two.

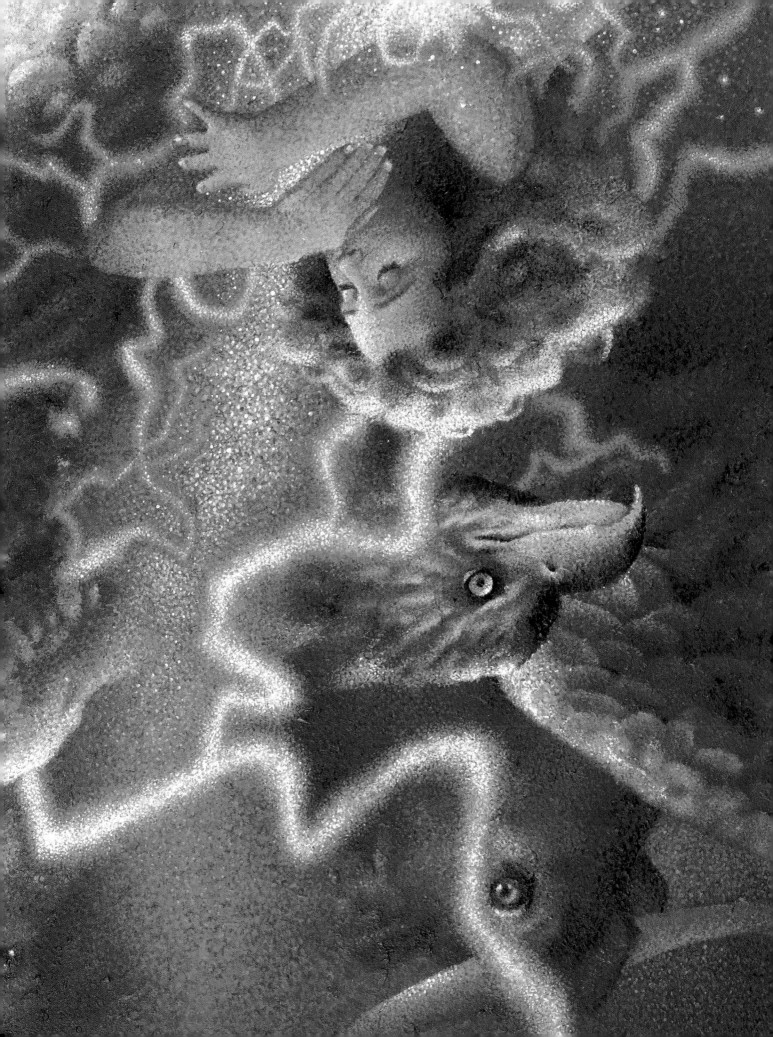

From horse into wolf, from wolf into boar, the enchanted Tamlin changed. Sometimes the wings of a golden eagle battered in Janet's face, and sometimes large flapping fins. But she did not loose her grip whether her fingers clung to tusks or antennae, pincers or curling horns. Somewhere, a clock struck three.

All night Janet held tight to Tamlin, though the
Fairy Queen changed him into all the horrors
of Hallowe'en: a ghoul, a boggart, a demon.
At last the gauzy ghostie in her arms
turned stiff and hard and heavy - turned
not to beast or monster, not to bird or
fish - but into an iron bar. And the iron
bar sang with heat.

Red hot, then white hot it glowed, ringing
with heat, soughing with the sound of the
blacksmith's forge.
　　　Though she thought she would be burned
to ashes, Janet did not let her enchanted
sweetheart drop into the roadway, but held
the bar tight to her body crying, "You may
burn hot, but my love burns hotter,
and I will NEVER let you go."
Somewhere a clock struck four.

The pale light of day made the horizon
shine like wire. And the Fairy Queen cursed aloud
to find her magic fading.

"Come, men! We must be gone. For today is All Hallows,
when the saints and angels ride out!" Pointing a malicious finger
she cried, "A curse on you, Plain Janet, and an ill death may you
die! For you have stolen the best man in my company!" Then sink-
ing her spurs into her elfin horse, she raced her outriders back over
the scarlet borders of Fairyland.

Softer and softer grew the bar in Janet's arms. And she found
she was holding Tamlin, pale and shivering,
dew-wet and muddy, asleep and asleep
and sound asleep.

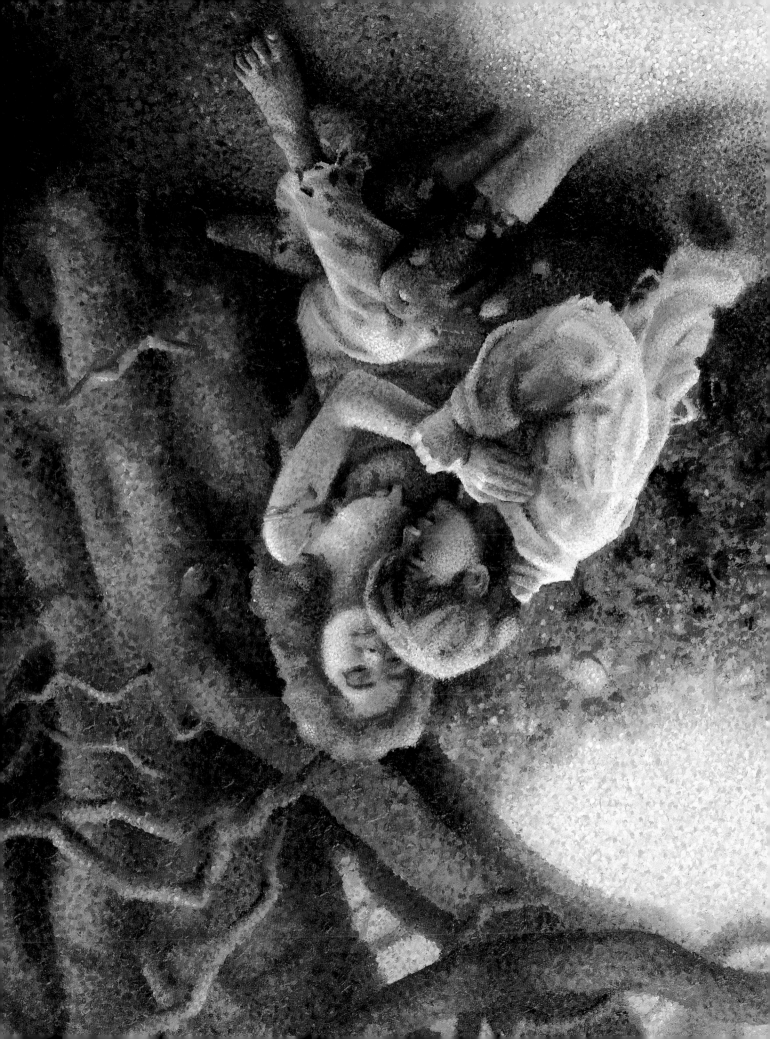

Even after his time in Fairyland, Tamlin of Carterhaugh was as handsome as any in Fairyland or the sunlit world. On the Christmas Day he and Janet got married, princesses in five counties wrung their hands and wondered: "He might have married me. So why did he marry *her*?"

But Tamlin no longer wondered. As he said, when he raised a toast to his bride, "I am the luckiest of men. I have found myself the best wife in the world and, by all that's good, I mean never to let her go!"

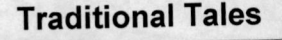

FOR THE SCOTTISH FAERY
G.M.

TO LISA, LOVE J
J.C.

Text copyright © Geraldine McCaughrean 1998
Illustrations copyright © Jason Cockcroft 1998

The right of Geraldine McCaughrean and Jason Cockcroft to be identified
as the author and illustrator of the Work has been asserted by them in
accordance with the Copyright, Designs and Patents Act 1988.

Published 1998 by Hodder Children's Books,
a division of Hodder Headline plc,
London NW1 3BH

10 9 8 7 6 5 4 3 2 1

ISBN 0 340 682914 (PB)
0 340 682906 (HB)

Printed in Hong Kong